1 84121 240 7

1 84121 238 5

Open wide, Wilbur!

1 84121 248 2

1 84121 256 3

1 84121 236 9

1 84121 246 6

1 84121 230 X

1 84121 234 2

1 84121 254 7

Colour CRACKERS

Read all the Colour CRACKERS books!

A Medal for Poppy
The Pluckiest Pig in the World!
Rose Impey and Shoo Rayner
1 84121 244 X

Too Many Babies
The Largest Litter in the World!
Rose Impey and Shoo Rayner
1 84121 242 3

Hot Dog Harris
The Smallest Dog in the World!
Rose Impey and Shoo Rayner
1 84121 232 6

Rhode Island Roy
The Roughest Rooster in the World!
Rose Impey and Shoo Rayner
1 84121 252 0

Welcome Home, Barney
The Loneliest Bat in the World!
Rose Impey and Shoo Rayner
1 84121 258 X

Pipe Down, Prudle!
The Most Talkative Parrot in the World!
Rose Impey and Shoo Rayner
1 84121 250 4

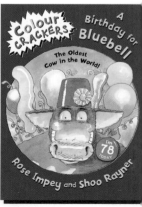

A Birthday for Bluebell
The Oldest Cow in the World!
Rose Impey and Shoo Rayner
1 84121 228 8

Open Wide Wilbur

The Most Welcoming Whale in the World!

Rose Impey
Shoo Rayner

ORCHARD BOOKS

ORCHARD BOOKS
96 Leonard Street, London EC2A 4XD
Orchard Books Australia
32/45-51 Huntley Street, Alexandria, NSW 2015
First published in Great Britain in 1997
This edition published in hardback in 2003
This edition published in paperback in 2003
Text © Rose Impey 1997
Illustrations © Shoo Rayner 2003
The rights of Rose Impey to be identified as the author
and Shoo Rayner as the illustrator of this work
have been asserted by them in accordance with the
Copyright, Designs and Patents Act, 1988.
A CIP catalogue record for this book is
available from the British Library.
ISBN 1 84121 884 7 (hardback)
ISBN 1 84121 248 2 (paperback)
1 3 5 7 9 10 8 6 4 2 (hardback)
3 5 7 9 10 8 6 4 2 (paperback)
Printed in Hong Kong

Open Wide Wilbur

Wilbur was a whopper of a whale.
His head was huge.
His mouth was massive.
And his stomach was *stupendous!*
In fact, it was so big
it could hold a complete world inside.

All day long Wilbur swam in the sea
with his mouth wide open,
looking for food.
But all the fishes knew that it was
safe to swim right in.
Wilbur was their friend;
he wouldn't hurt them.
He was the most welcoming whale
in the world.

"Wipe your fins and come on in,"
he said, with a nice wide grin.

Wilbur liked helping his friends.
He was happy to give them a ride.
When Willy Whiting was late for work
he often hitched a lift with Wilbur.

When Hattie Haddock wanted
a holiday, Wilbur took her
all the way to Disney World.
And brought her home again.

And when old Tom Tuna was too
tired to visit his family and friends,
Wilbur brought *them* to see *him*.

Wilbur was so big and so strong,
a few more fish didn't worry him.
He just swam harder.
"It's always good to help," he said,
with a nod of his huge, kind head.

Wilbur's friends came
in all shapes and sizes:
conger eel, cod and crab,

baby dolphins, dogfish and dab.

Perch and plaice and pole,

swordfish, stingray and sole.

They all knew that *Wilbur's Place*
was the very best place to be
if you wanted to
meet your friends,
or hear the latest gossip,
or find out the fishing news.

Sometimes there were so many fish
riding in Wilbur's stomach,
he felt weighed down.
But Wilbur didn't complain.
He just swam harder.
"What else are friends for?"
he said with a smile.
"It's only for a little while."

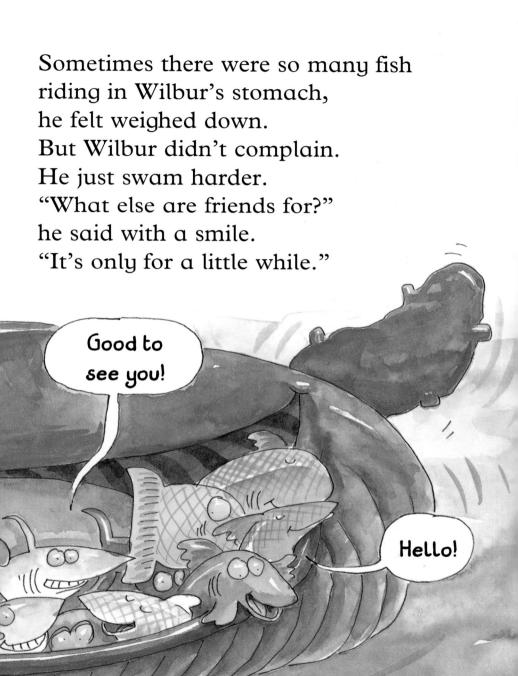

But Wilbur was too kind
and too welcoming
for his own good.
Some of his visitors decided
to stay and set up home.
They moved in their families
and friends
and all their furniture.
It was like a little fish world,
right there in Wilbur's stomach.

The fish had everything they needed.
There was even a school
for the baby fishes,
with teachers and nursemaids
to look after them.

Wilbur couldn't turn anyone away.
He didn't like to say,
"Sorry, no room. Full to the tail.
You'll have to catch the next whale."

But when Wilbur was full up
the fish who were living inside him
began to complain.

They sent the Fighting Fishes
to stand guard in Wilbur's mouth
and frighten the new fish away.

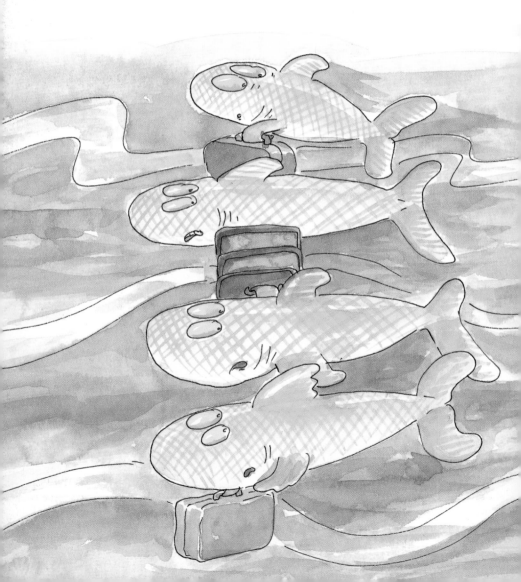

The fish had no need to go out.
Wilbur caught enough food
for everyone.
As it passed through his stomach,
they just helped themselves.
They soon grew fat and lazy,
floating around all day,
doing nothing.

Even when there wasn't much food
left for him,
Wilbur didn't complain.
But the fish inside Wilbur complained.
They complained all the time.

The fish even complained
about each other.
The herrings were very hoity-toity;
they looked down on the dogfish.

The skate were stuck up
and wouldn't speak to the squid.

The flounders were always
falling out with the other flatfish.

And when all the baby brill started crying, it gave Grandma Hake one of her headaches.

Sometimes the arguments upset Wilbur.
He felt tired and sad.
"You try to do your best," he said,
"but it's never enough."

And he shook his head.

As time went on, Wilbur had to
travel further and further,
and
dive
deeper
and
deeper,
to
find
enough
food
for
everyone.

Then, one day, disaster struck.
Wilbur was swimming
close to the surface.
He swam close to a huge boat.
It was a fishing boat.
The fishermen spotted Wilbur.
They started to chase him.

Wilbur swam as fast as he could,
but he was tired and heavy.
He couldn't swim fast enough
to escape.

The boat was coming closer
and closer.
Wilbur's heart was beating fast
and his brain was trying to
think what to do.
But it was hard to think
with everyone inside him
complaining.

But Wilbur couldn't even
save himself.
There was only one thing to do.

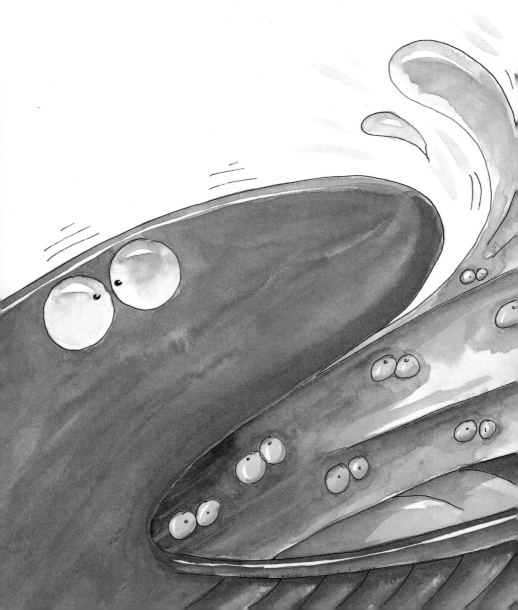

Wilbur lifted his huge head
and opened his massive mouth
as wide as it would go.
He blew out a *stupendous*
stream of water
and out came all the fish
and all their families.

They flew up in the air
and landed in the water.
There were flying fishes
everywhere.

The fishermen could easily
have caught them,
but they only wanted Wilbur.
They kept on chasing him.

But now, Wilbur was so light
and so fast,
he swam away across the ocean.
He led the boat away from his friends
who swam to safety.

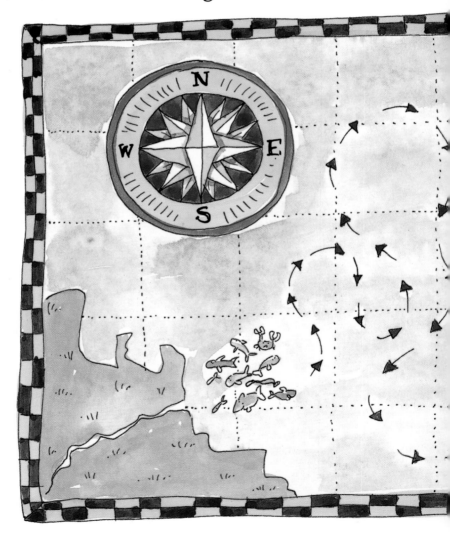

Wilbur travelled a very long way
before he escaped;
hundreds of miles away
from all his friends.

For a while he felt a little lonely.
But it wasn't long before
Wilbur made new friends.
Lots and lots and lots of friends.

Because, after all, he was
the most welcoming whale
in the world.

Crack-A-Joke

What zooms along the sea bed on three wheels? **A motorpike and sidecarp!**

What sleeps at the bottom of the sea? **A kipper!**

 Z ZZZZZ Z

Why are fish so easy to weigh? **Because they've got their own scales!**

What's the difference between a fish and a piano? **You can't tuna fish!**

Why did the sea roar? **Because it had crabs on its bottom!**

Having a whale of a time!

What did the mummy sardine say
when a submarine passed by?
Don't worry. It's only a tin of people!

What does the ocean say
when it sees the shore?
Nothing. . . it just waves!

Where would you weigh a whale?

At a whale-weigh station!

There are 16 Colour Crackers books.
Collect them all!

❏ A Birthday for Bluebell	1 84121 228 8	£3.99
❏ A Fortune for Yo-Yo	1 84121 230 X	£3.99
❏ A Medal for Poppy	1 84121 244 X	£3.99
❏ Hot Dog Harris	1 84121 232 6	£3.99
❏ Long Live Roberto	1 84121 246 6	£3.99
❏ Open Wide, Wilbur	1 84121 248 2	£3.99
❏ Phew, Sidney!	1 84121 234 2	£3.99
❏ Pipe Down, Prudle!	1 84121 250 4	£3.99
❏ Precious Potter	1 84121 236 9	£3.99
❏ Rhode Island Roy	1 84121 252 0	£3.99
❏ Sleepy Sammy	1 84121 238 5	£3.99
❏ Stella's Staying Put	1 84121 254 7	£3.99
❏ Tiny Tim	1 84121 240 7	£3.99
❏ Too Many Babies	1 84121 242 3	£3.99
❏ We Want William!	1 84121 256 3	£3.99
❏ Welcome Home, Barney	1 84121 258 X	£3.99

Colour Crackers are available from all good bookshops,
or can be ordered direct from the publisher:
Orchard Books, PO BOX 29, Douglas IM99 1BQ
Credit card orders please telephone 01624 836000 or fax 01624 837033
or e-mail: bookshop@enterprise.net for details.
To order please quote title, author and ISBN and your full name and address.
Cheques and postal orders should be made payable to 'Bookpost plc'.
Postage and packing is FREE within the UK
(overseas customers should add £1.00 per book).
Prices and availability are subject to change.

1 84121 244 X

1 84121 240 7

1 84121 238 5

1 84121 252 0

1 84121 256 3

1 84121 236 9

1 84121 228 8

1 84121 230 X

1 84121 234 2

1 84121 248 2

1 84121 242 3

1 84121 232 6

1 84121 246 6

1 84121 258 X

1 84121 250 4

1 84121 254 7

Collect all the
Colour Crackers!